W9-BXX-799

Look for these
ROTTEN SCHOOL
books, too!

ROTTEN SCHOOL

GROWTH LEARNING PIZZA!

PARTY POOPERS

R.L. STINE

Illustrations by Trip Park

HarperCollins*Publishers*

A Parachute Press Book

For Grandottie
–TP

Library of Congress Cataloging-in-Publication Data is available.
ISBN-10: 0-06-078824-0 (trade bdg.)—ISBN-10: 0-06-078825-9 (lib. bdg.)
ISBN-13: 978-0-06-078824-7 (trade bdg.)—ISBN-13: 978-0-06-078825-4 (lib. bdg.)

Cover and interior design by mjcdesign
1 2 3 4 5 6 7 8 9 10

First Edition

CONTENTS

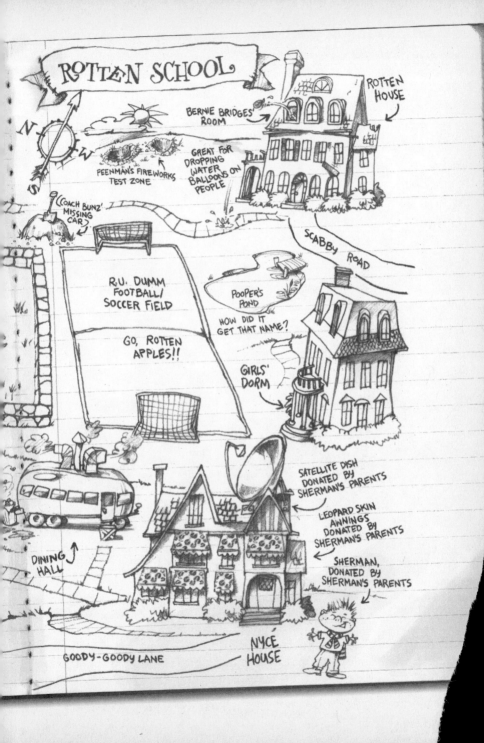

MORNING ANNOUNCEMENTS

Good morning, Rotten students. This is Headmaster Upchuck. I'd like to begin our Rotten day by reading the Morning Announcements. Those of you who are screaming or crying at the top of your lungs or pounding each other with your fists—please *stop* so that others may hear the announcements. Thank you.

● The fourth grader known as Beast would like to invite everyone to the Crafts Fair in the gym. When

1

you go, you can see Beast's life-size sculpture of *me*—Headmaster Upchuck—made entirely from things he found in his nose.

Students in Ms. Sally Monella's Homemaker class will be selling used baked goods at the Crafts Fair. Ms. Monella tells me the cookies, brownies, and cakes are only *slightly* used.

I'm sorry to say that the Butt Sculptures molded in clay by third grader Murray Krissmus are disgusting and will not be shown at the fair. Murray's clay has been taken away from him.

Mrs. Twinkler announces something exciting this week: The guest speaker on Guest Speaker Day will be a well-known Hollywood chimpanzee.

And finally, fifth grader Harry Ahrms has been sent home for a while. He knows why.

Chapter 1

GO, BERNIE!

The sun was shining. Birds twittered in the apple trees. As I trotted across the sparkling, green lawn, I sang to myself, my new favorite song....

"I love Bernie Bridges,
Bernie is the one who has fun.
Go, Bernie! Go, Bernie!
La-duh-da-duh-da whatever rhymes with Bridges."

Yes, I was making it up as I went along. I always write songs in my head. And they're usually about one of my favorite people in the whole world—ME.

Come on, dudes—if *you* were popular and good-looking and smart—who would *you* sing about?

And today I had a *lot* to sing about.

For one thing, I love being at Rotten School. You poor thing. You probably have to go home every day after school. But Rotten School is a boarding school. I get to live at school in a dorm with all my friends—and NO PARENTS!

Cool enough for you?

Another reason I was singing: I was on my way to the girls' dorm to find April-May June. April-May June is the hottest, coolest, dreamiest, drooliest, babe-alicious girl on campus.

She's my girlfriend. Only she doesn't know it yet. She doesn't have a *clue* that we were meant for each other. But she *definitely* can't resist me.

Who can resist Bernie B.?

"Go, Bernie!
Go, Bernie!

La-la-la something that rhymes with Bernie..."

Don't you wish *you* could write songs off the top of your head like that?

Another reason I was singing? It was almost time for the party of the year. The All-Nighter. One of the great Rotten School traditions. Maybe you guessed from the name—the party goes ALL NIGHT LONG! We don't go to sleep till the sun comes up.

"Go, Bernie! Go, Bernie!"

I knew April-May wanted to spend that special night with only one special person—Bernie B.

So I was trotting across the Great Lawn. I sang to myself and watched the girls come out of their tall, white dorm.

5

Suddenly I heard a deafening cry behind me:

"DUCK! BERNIE— DUCK!!"

Huh?
I stopped singing and hit the ground hard.

Chapter 2

DUCK PLOP

"OOF!"

I landed on my stomach. My breath shot out in a painful *whoosh!* With a groan, I spun around and glanced behind me.

I saw my friend Feenman running across the grass. He was hugging a big, brown duck in his arms. The duck was quacking its head off and snapping at Feenman's ears.

"Duck, Bernie!" he shouted.

I pushed myself to my feet. I brushed off the

knees of my khakis. "Feenman," I said, "where did you get that duck?"

"I found it," he said.

The duck honked and chewed off a big hunk of Feenman's brown hair.

"You'd better set it free," I said. "It doesn't like you."

Feenman's mouth dropped open. "Set it free? But I *found* it! It's mine!"

Feenman is not the brightest candle on the cake. If we are talking brains, the duck would win.

Feenman squeezed the duck a little too hard. It dropped a disgusting mess onto his shoes.

"Bernie, are you going to the hard-boiled-egg-eating contest Friday?" Feenman asked. "Are you gonna bet on Beast?"

Our friend Beast can eat anything. Last year he ate *forty-two* hard-boiled eggs before he barfed his guts out.

I made a *ton* of money betting on the dude.

"I don't have time for the contest," I said. "I've got to find April-May. I want to go with her to the All-Nighter."

"It's a girl-ask-boy party," Feenman said. "If a girl doesn't ask you, you can't go!"

"April-May is *desperate* to ask me," I said. "She just doesn't know it yet."

The duck snapped off another hunk of Feenman's hair. "Did you hear what they are planning?" he asked. "A huge barbeque. A soccer game on R.U. Dumm Field—boys against girls. Then a three-legged race across Pooper's Pond. And a treasure hunt in the dark for BIG prizes."

I rubbed my hands together. "I gotta get to that party," I said. "I have a special reason. I'll show you why."

I saw my buddy Belzer staggering under the two huge cartons he was carrying for me. You don't expect Bernie B. to carry two fifty-pound cartons, do you?

"Belzer—come over here!" I shouted.

He stumbled forward. "Hunh-hunh-hunh." He was gasping for breath. "Hunh-hunh." Sweat poured off his pudgy face.

"Okay. You can set 'em down for a minute," I said.

Belzer lowered the cartons. Then he fell face-down onto the grass in a dead faint.

"Feenman, put down the duck," I said. "Check this out."

He hugged the duck tighter. "Maybe we can cook it," he said.

"Feenman, we're kids—remember? Kids don't cook duck."

He nodded. "Yeah. You're right. I don't wanna eat duck, anyway. All those feathers would get stuck in my teeth."

"Drop it," I said. "Before *it* drops another pile of plop onto your shoes."

Oops. Too late.

Feenman finally opened his arms and set the duck free. It tore across the grass, flapping and squawking.

"Feenman, come over here," I said. I tugged open one of the cartons. "This is why I've gotta get to the All-Nighter. Check this out...."

Chapter 3

MY BIGGEST FAULT

Feenman squinted into the open carton. "What are those, Big B?"

I pulled out one of the shiny, red objects. "Pocket flashlights," I said. "Two hundred pocket flashlights."

He stared at the one in my hand. "For seeing into your pocket?"

I rolled my eyes. "No, Feenman. They're for *cheating* at the treasure hunt. It's gonna be pitch black at night, right? Well...every kid at the party will want one."

Feenman pulled a flashlight from the box and studied it. "For finding the hidden treasure?"

"You got it," I said. "I'm gonna sell them cheap. Only a dollar each. I'll sell all two hundred. Easy. This party is gonna make me RICH!"

Feenman clicked the flashlight on. He frowned at it and clicked it again. "Bernie," he said, "this flashlight doesn't work."

"You've got to slap it a few times," I said. "What do you *want* for a dollar?"

Feenman slapped the end of the flashlight, and the light flickered on. "Cool," he said. "What's in the other box?"

I tugged open the carton and pulled out a sweatshirt. "You know how cold it gets late at night. I'm gonna sell at *least* a hundred of these—at five dollars each."

"Wow," Feenman said. "Let me see the front."

I held up the sweatshirt. It had a big picture of my smiling face on it. And it read: I PARTIED ALL NIGHT WITH BERNIE!

"Feenman," I said, "can anyone *resist* a sweatshirt like this? Of course not."

I folded up the sweatshirt and dropped it back into the carton. "Kids will also want to buy the flashlights so they can see their new sweatshirts! It's a perfect combo!"

"Brilliant!" Feenman cried. "Bernie, you're a genius!"

"We'll be rich. RICH!" I cried. "All of us dudes at Rotten House—we'll be *rolling* in money! Of course, I'm only doing this for my guys."

Feenman scratched his head. "You mean you're gonna share the money with us?"

"Maybe five or ten dollars," I said. "Don't thank me, Feenman. I know I'm *too generous*. It's my biggest fault."

I dragged Belzer to his feet. "Take the boxes to the dorm," I said. "And be careful with them. I spent *three months'* allowance on this stuff."

"Hunh-hunh." Belzer staggered off with the cartons. Good kid, Belzer.

Feenman shook his head. "Bernie, you spent three months' allowance? What if no girl asks you to the All-Nighter? You're totally *sunk*."

I put a hand on his shoulder. "Are you kidding? A

dozen girls are *dying* to ask me. Maybe *two* dozen. But they're holding themselves back. Because they know April-May June wants to ask me first."

And then I saw her crossing the grass. I saw her blond ponytail bobbing in the sunlight. Her blue eyes sparkling, her mouth in a happy smile.

Was she thinking about *me*?

"Take a lesson, Feenman," I said. "Watch how I allow April-May to ask me to the party."

I took off, trotting to catch up to her.

Chapter 4

THREE NOSTRILS?

"April-May—hi!" I called. "Wait up!"

She kept walking. I guess she didn't hear me.

"Wait up!"

She walked a little faster. She probably didn't know it was me.

I had to run full speed. I caught up with her and spun her around. I flashed her my most adorable smile, the one with the dimples. "Hi ya, babes. Whussup?"

She gave me a warm greeting. "Take a hike, Pond Scum."

I laughed. "Did anyone ever tell you that you have an awesome sense of humor?"

She pulled a fat wad of pink bubble gum from her mouth and stuck it onto my forehead.

I know what it means when girls tease you that way. It means *they really like you!*

"April-May, you look totally excellent today," I said.

"You look like the breakfast I just threw up," she replied.

I laughed again. "Funny. I love a good laugh in the morning."

"Want a good laugh, Bernie? Go look in a mirror!" she said.

I had to run again to catch up to her. I knew all her hard-to-get tricks.

"You're so shy," I said. "Don't be ashamed. I'm shy, too."

She pulled the bubble gum off my forehead and shoved it back into her mouth.

"I know how much you want to ask me to the All-Nighter," I said. "So don't be shy. Just go ahead and ask me."

She rolled her beautiful eyes. "I'd rather have big, red pimples up and down my tongue," she said.

"Is that a *yes?*" I asked.

"I'd rather stick my head into Pooper's Pond," she

18

said. "I'd rather drill a third nostril into my nose."

"Is that a maybe?" I asked. I slapped my hand over her mouth. "No. Don't answer. I know what you're really saying. You're *really* saying you want to ask me to the All-Nighter."

April-May tossed back her head and laughed until she swallowed her bubble gum.

"OWW!" I let out a scream as someone attacked me from behind.

I felt two strong arms wrap around my waist. I lurched—and fell backward onto the grass. Before I could move, someone landed on my stomach.

Jennifer Ecch!

That big, hulking girl I call Nightmare Girl. She sat on me, her stringy hair falling over her face. She gazed down at me with her one brown eye and one blue eye.

"Honey Cakes," she cooed, "guess who's going to the All-Nighter with me?"

Chapter 5

BERNIE BREATH

Do you know how *embarrassing* it is to be in fourth grade and have a girl who's totally in love with you?

Jennifer Ecch follows me everywhere. She calls me Honey Cakes and Baby Lamb. She thinks it's perfectly okay to plant loud, smoochy kisses all over me—even in class!

It's hard to fight her. She's big and strong. She opens cans with her *teeth*!

And now here she was, sitting on my chest, inviting me to the All-Nighter *in front of my girlfriend*!

I struggled to breathe. "April-May, don't be

jealous," I choked out.

April-May laughed. "That's so adorable, the way Jennifer tackled you and knocked your breath out," she said.

"Adorable?" I cried. "She broke sixteen ribs!"

April-May grinned down at me. "That's so cute, the way Jennifer is planting smoochy kisses up and down your arm."

I groaned. "It's giving me a skin rash! I'll have to see the nurse!"

Jennifer grabbed my head and tugged it.

"The head doesn't come off!" I screamed. "It's attached to my neck!"

April-May laughed again. "Bernie, it's so totally cute how she's got you in that headlock and won't let go until you agree to go to the All-Nighter with her!"

"Cute? You call this *cute?*" I wailed. "She rubbed off all my hair. I've been *scalped!*"

April-May shrugged. "Frankly, Bernie, I don't know what she sees in you." She tossed back her blond ponytail and hurried away.

The Ecch leaned over me, breaking a few more ribs. "Don't pay any attention to that stuck-up girl,

Lamby Toes," she cooed.

"Don't call me Lamby Toes!" I shouted.

"Baa-baa Berniekins," she said.

SICK!

"Jennifer, I . . . I can't go with you to the All-Nighter."

She gave my ears a hard tug. I knew my earmuffs wouldn't fit anymore. "Why not?" she demanded.

"I ... I have Dorm Patrol that night. I have to stay in and guard the dorm."

She pulled my ears again. This time she pulled them so hard, they touched each other! "Honey Face, there's no such thing as Dorm Patrol."

I gulped. "There isn't?"

She squeezed my neck until my eyeballs nearly popped out. "Bernie Breath, we'll have so much fun at the All-Nighter!"

"Please—*please* don't call me Bernie Breath!" I begged.

"We'll have the whole night together!" she said. "Hours and hours!"

I groaned. I knew what the night would be like. Jennifer hugging me and holding on to me and calling me Bernie Breath in front of all my friends.

Yuck!

I mean, double Yuck!

I *couldn't* go with Jennifer. No way. Especially since April-May was *dying* to ask me!

And here was the other problem: If The Ecch was hugging me all night, how would I sell my sweat-shirts and flashlights?

I spent three months' allowance on that stuff. I *had* to sell it all!

That meant I had to get to the party—*without* Jennifer!

But—how?

Chapter 6

THE COOLEST DUDE

Wes Updood lives across the Great Lawn from us in Nyce House—the dorm we Rotten House dudes all hate. But that doesn't matter—Wes is the coolest guy on campus.

He is tall and thin and has spiky, brown hair. I don't know what color eyes he has because he never takes off his shades—even in the shower!

Wes plays saxophone and has an awesome rock band. He's so totally cool, no one can understand a *word* he says!

After classes, I went to the gym to help Coach

Manley Bunz deflate the basketballs. Coach likes to take all the air out of the balls after every practice. Don't ask me why.

I was surprised to see Wes in the middle of the floor, practicing with his band. He lowered his big, golden sax and flipped me a two-fingered salute.

"Whussup, dude?" Wes Updood said.

"Not much," I said. "What's up with the band? Are you gonna play at the All-Nighter?"

Wes nodded. "Like wrinkles on a prune," he said. "Pure sponge cake."

See what I mean? You've got to be as cool as Wes to understand him. What was he trying to tell me? "Pure sponge cake?" I said.

Wes frowned at me. "Don't go there." He blew a note on his sax. It echoed off the gym walls.

I tried again. "So your band is gonna play at the party?"

"No way," Wes said. "Way. I mean, what if you swallow a cherry pit? Grow with it, right? A mind is a terrible thing to *use*. Know what I mean?"

"Well...not exactly..."

"Blueberries aren't really berries, are they?

They're alive, man. ALIVE! Ever watch 'em move around on your tongue?"

"Well—"

"Watch their little faces. They turn blue if you look at them."

"Really?"

"Now you're gettin' it! Pure sponge cake!" he cried again. He slapped me a high five. Then we touched knuckles. He blew another high note on his sax that rattled the windows.

"Wes, has a girl asked you to the party?" I asked.

"Shake well before drinking. Don't spit into the wind. King Kong, y'all." Wes gave me another two-fingered salute. Then he turned to his band, and they started to play a loud, hard-rocking song.

I walked off shaking my head. I wished I was as cool as Wes. Wes is such an awesome dude.

I turned and saw Jennifer Ecch watching from the bleachers. The girl is SICK. She follows me wherever I go.

"Pure sponge cake!" Wes Updood called to her.

"Cream filling!" she shouted back.

WHOA. Did Jennifer *understand* Wes?

I blinked. An awesome idea popped into my head. So awesome, I felt dizzy.

What if I could get Jennifer Ecch to have a crush on Wes?

Suddenly I had a plan. A plan to lose Nightmare Girl.

I saw Coach Bunz starting to deflate the basketballs. I hurried across the gym to help him.

But I knew what I had to do. I had to see April-May's good friend, Sharonda Davis, right away!

Chapter 7

THE SOUND THE SHARKS MAKE

Sharonda Davis is the biggest gossip at Rotten School. That's why I had to see her first.

I found her watching TV in the media room at the Student Center. It was *Shark Week* on the Discovery Channel—and Sharonda was cheering for the sharks!

That's cold, right?

Sharonda is tall and thin, with chocolate-colored skin, big, brown eyes, and black hair that she wears in a single braid down her back.

She's a lot like her friend April-May in one way.

She also *pretends* she doesn't like me very much. Of course, it's just an act.

Time to put my plan into action. I slumped back and forth in front of Sharonda, moaning and shaking my head.

"Don't get in my way," Sharonda said. "In a few minutes the shark eats a swimmer. I've seen this episode. It's totally great."

I pretended not to hear her. "Sigh, sigh," I said. I moped back and forth, looking as sad and worried as I could.

"Don't make so much noise," Sharonda said, tucking her long legs beneath her on the couch. "I like the sound the shark makes when it's chewing on someone."

Sweet, huh?

"Sigh, sigh," I said again.

Sharonda rolled her eyes. "Okay, Bernie. What's your problem?"

I shook my head sadly and let a tear roll down my cheek.

"Why are you acting so pitiful?" Sharonda asked.

"It's Jennifer," I said, making my voice shake.

"What about her?" Sharonda said. "Did she beat you at arm wrestling again?"

"No," I replied. "It's just ... well ... I'm not good enough for her."

Sharonda jumped up from the couch. "You got THAT right!" she said.

I sniffled and wiped away the tear. "I know," I said. "I'm just a big loser. Jennifer is so awesome. She deserves someone better."

"Smartest thing you ever said!" Sharonda replied.

"Jennifer should ask someone *cool* to the All-Nighter," I said. "She shouldn't take me. She needs someone cool—like Wes Updood."

I got up on tiptoes and whispered into Sharonda's ear. "Can I tell you a secret?"

Her eyes lit up. She *lives* for secrets! "Yeah, sure," she said.

"Promise you won't tell anyone?"

She nodded. "I won't tell a soul. Promise."

"Double promise?" I said. "It's a *big* secret."

"Double promise," Sharonda agreed. She made a zipping motion across her lips. "I won't tell."

"Wes Updood told me he has a *total crush* on

Jennifer," I whispered.

Sharonda swallowed. "Really?"

I nodded. "Don't tell," I said. "I know I don't deserve Jennifer. Please don't tell her."

"Don't worry about it," Sharonda said.

I hunched my shoulders, sighed a few times, and slumped out of the Student Center. Outside, I hid behind a tree and waited.

Two minutes later Sharonda came
running out. I knew where she
was going. I followed her.
Sharonda headed straight
for April-May.

April-May sat behind a card table near the statue of our school's founder, Mr. I. B. Rotten. She had two big signs next to the table. They both read: HELP SAVE THE CHIMPANZEES.

What chimpanzees? And *what* was she saving them from?

I didn't know. But she had a big jar half-filled with money that kids had given her.

I hid behind another tree to spy on Sharonda and April-May. But I couldn't keep my eyes off that money jar. If I had a big, black marker I could change the signs to read: HELP SAVE BERNIE BRIDGES. . . .

I forced my eyes away from the jar. Sure enough, Sharonda was telling April-May my secret.

Am I a genius, or am I a genius?

My plan to de-Jennifer myself was under way!

Chapter 8

TOE FUNGUS

Sharonda tugged April-May to her feet. She pulled April-May away. I knew where they were going—off to find Jennifer.

I crept to the table. *The chimps won't mind if I borrow a few dollars from them,* I thought. But, sadly, April-May took the money jar with her.

I followed the two girls to the exercise room. I waited a minute or two, then sneaked in after them. I ducked behind a stationary bike.

Jennifer was lifting a girl who was lifting weights.

I know it's hard to picture. But that's how strong

The Ecch is. Pumping fifty-pound weights is too easy. She likes to lift a hundred-pound *person* who is pumping fifty-pound weights.

A shiver ran down my back. I suddenly pictured Jennifer showing off—holding me over her head, raising me up and down in front of everyone.

I had to get rid of her. My LIFE was at stake!

I leaned forward and listened to their conversation.

"Bernie is a total creep," Sharonda told Jennifer. "Even he *himself* said you deserve someone better."

Jennifer groaned as she lifted the girl lifting the weights. "Bernie is so modest," she said. "He's so cute. What a sweet thing for him to say."

"You're not getting it," Sharonda said. "He said you deserve someone better than him. Someone cool. Like Wes Updood."

Jennifer giggled. "That's so totally sweet. Bernie can't help himself. He's just so adorable!"

She set the weight girl down. "Thanks for the workout," she said. "But I need someone a little heavier." The girl staggered away.

I shivered and shuddered. Why did the strongest nine-year-old girl on the planet pick *me* to be her boyfriend?

"You should ask Wes Updood to the All-

Nighter," April-May told Jennifer.

"No way," Jennifer replied, toweling off her face. "I couldn't disappoint Bernie that way. It would break his heart."

Go ahead. Break my heart, I thought. *Please!*

Sharonda had her arms crossed in front of her. She shook her head. "You really deserve someone better," she said.

"Yes," April-May agreed. "What if we prove to you that Bernie is just toe fungus?"

Perfect! I thought. *That's me. Toe fungus. Jennifer, LISTEN to them!*

The Ecch giggled. "You girls are teasing me, right? You both know how wonderful my Honey Cakes is!"

Sharonda stuck a finger down her throat and made gagging sounds.

I told you: She pretends she doesn't like me.

"What if we *prove* it to you?" April-May asked Jennifer again. "What if we prove to you that Bernie is a creep and a loser? Then will you drop him?"

The Ecch giggled again. "Lamby Knees? A creep and a loser? No way!"

Okay. I knew what I had to do.

I had to act like a creep and a loser.

It wouldn't be easy for someone as handsome and popular and smart as me. But I could do it.

To convince Jennifer to drop me, I could be toe fungus. I could be the biggest creep and loser at Rotten School.

Just watch me!

Chapter 9

CRYBABIES

"Okay, dudes—get your butts over here!"

Ever try to round up a group of first graders?

The little guys were wrestling on the grass and tackling one another, fighting and shouting and pushing and poking one another's eyes out.

Totally cute.

"Dudes—get over here!" I shouted. I pulled two wrestling kids to their feet, one in each hand.

"Yo—what's that? Give it! Give!" I grabbed a Nutty-Nutty candy bar from a kid who was stuffing his face.

"How many times do I have to tell you kids to eat *healthy*? Eat *healthy*!" I shoved the candy bar into my mouth to keep the kid from ruining his lunch.

As an older student, I have to set an example. "Okay, everyone line up!" I shouted.

A chubby kid with red hair and a faceful of freckles stuck his tongue out at me.

"Come over here, kid," I said. "What's your name?"

He sneered at me. "I don't know. I'm only in first grade!"

"Ha-ha. A joker!" I said. "You'll go far, kid. Do you know how to spell NOT FUNNY?"

He shook his head. "No. We haven't done spelling yet."

I *liked* this kid. He reminded me of ME.

But I didn't have time for jokers. I knew that April-May, Sharonda, and Jennifer would be walking by here soon.

I herded the kids into the courtyard next to Rotten House, my dorm. The dorm is a beat-up old house with shingles falling off and a leaky roof. But we love it.

I pointed up to a window on the third floor. "That's my room up there," I told them.

"Is that a big whoop-de-doo?" the freckled kid said. "I mean, are we supposed to care?"

"Ha-ha." I laughed and pinched his cheek. Okay. Maybe I pinched a little too hard. The redness would go away in a week or two.

"Listen up, dudes!" I shouted. "I brought you guys here to play a little game."

"YEAAAA!"

Some of them cheered and slapped high fives. Others just stared at me.

I checked my watch. Almost time.

"Here's what I'm gonna do," I said. "I'm gonna go up to my room on the third floor and drop water balloons onto your heads."

"YEAAAA!"

They cheered again.

"And I want you guys to cry," I said. "When I hit you with a water balloon, I want you to cry really loudly and sob your eyes out."

The redheaded kid stepped forward. "But we LIKE to have water balloons dropped on us!" he said.

I pinched his other cheek. "I know you like it," I said. "But this is a game. I want you to be the biggest crybabies on campus—get it? I want you to pretend that I'm a mean dude, and you *hate* it."

They shook their heads, looking confused.

I checked my watch again. "Just do it," I said. "Cry your eyes out. Make it look really sad—okay?"

I ran into the house. I shot up the stairs to my room and pulled open the window. I could see the little dudes down there, huddled in a circle, talking it over.

My targets.

I had a basket of water balloons ready. Piece of cake!

I leaned out the window. "Get ready, guys!" I shouted down. "I wanna see *real* tears!"

From the third floor, I had a good view of the path from the Great Lawn. I knew the three girls would be walking by any minute now, on their way to the girls' dorm.

You want to see a creep?

You want to see a creep and a loser?

Bernie B. is your man!

Across the lawn I could see the three girls approaching. Another minute and they'd be here.

I picked up a fat water balloon in each hand, took a deep breath, and got ready for ACTION!

Chapter 10

SPLAT!

SPLAT! SPLAT! SPLOOOOSH!

As soon as April-May, Sharonda, and Jennifer came near, I let the water balloons drop. They made wonderful sounds as they exploded on the kids' heads.

"WAAAH! WAAAH!" The dudes started wailing and sobbing, just as I told them to.

"I'm drowning! I'm DROWNING!" the red-headed kid screamed. And I hadn't even *dropped* one on him yet! This kid was an *actor*!

SPLAT!

"WAAAAAH! I'm wet! I'm wet! SOB SOB!"

The first graders were soaked. Some of them dropped to their knees, crying and sobbing and rubbing their eyes.

The kids were *brilliant*!

I watched April-May and Sharonda shaking their heads. "Can you *believe* what Bernie is doing?" Sharonda cried to Jennifer.

"See how that creep treats those little kids?" April-May said. "Just for a mean laugh!"

SPLAT! SPLAT!

"WAAAAAH! He hit me! He hit me!

WAAAAH!"

I leaned out the window and shouted down at the girls. "This is totally FUN! Want to try it?" I tossed back my head and let out an evil laugh.

Sharonda grabbed Jennifer by the elbow. "See what we mean?" she cried. "See what a loser creep he is?"

SPLAAAAT!

"WAAAH! WAAAAH!"

Jennifer looked up and blew me a kiss. Then she turned back to Sharonda. "Oh, boys will be boys," she said. "Honey Cakes is just having a little fun."

Huh?

I sailed a few more fat balloons out the window. *SPLAT!* One of them dropped a kid to his knees. He started to sob.

"Bernie is so *unselfish*," Jennifer said. "He'd rather be with his friends. But here he is, sharing himself with the little kids. Teaching them about life. It's totally wonderful. They look up to him so much!"

She blew me ten or twenty more kisses.

Oh, wow.

Failure. Total failure.

Making the first graders cry didn't turn her against me at all. When I dropped water balloons onto their heads, it made her PROUD of me!

I shook my head. Getting rid of The Ecch was going to be a *lot* tougher than I thought.

But, hey, does the great Bernie B. give up after only one try?

I knew I could prove to Jennifer that I was a lowly worm who didn't deserve her.

Don't worry your head about *this* dude. I knew I could think up some other ideas that *totally* rocked!

Chapter 11

THE BIG RODENT HUNT

The next morning we had an assembly in the auditorium about the All-Nighter. Every seat was filled. Kids were laughing and talking. Belzer saved me a seat in the third row.

My friend Beast stood up in the aisle. Beast is a good guy, but no one really knows if he's animal or human. In class, Mrs. Heinie keeps him on a leash, which I don't think is fair.

Beast pulled off his school uniform shirt and started playing "America the Beautiful" on his armpit. The dude has armpit hair that goes down to

52

his waist. So it was pretty gross to look at him.

But *no one* can play armpit like Beast. He plays with so much enthusiasm and skill! He started squeezing out some rap beats with both armpits and had the whole auditorium boogying!

I looked up and saw Mr. and Mrs. Pocketlint walk onto the stage. They both had their hands pressed over their ears. They like classical stuff like Mozart and Beethoven. You could tell they don't care for armpit music.

The Pocketlints are the dorm parents in Nyce House. Mr. Pocketlint has a slender, pink face, a very long, pointed nose, and tiny, blue eyes, very close together. He looks a lot like one of those anteaters you see in cartoons.

His wife has gray hair piled high on her head. She has large, gray eyes and a big, snooty nose that always seems to be sniffing the air.

They waved their arms and shouted for us all to be quiet. It took a long time for everyone to calm down.

Beast took out a hairbrush and started brushing his armpit hair. He did it for a joke. And, of course, we all went wild, laughing and cheering him on.

But the Pocketlints didn't think armpit brushing was funny. Mr. Pocketlint slipped a dog leash onto Beast and led him out of the auditorium. We all booed and hissed.

A few minutes later everyone finally settled down. Mrs. Pocketlint sniffed the air. Her husband returned and took out a large, white handkerchief and blew his nose into the microphone. It sounded a lot like Beast's armpit music.

"We are the chaperones for the All-Nighter party," Mrs. P. announced. "That means Sam and I will be watching your every move, making sure you don't have as much fun as you'd like."

I think that was supposed to be a joke. But nobody laughed.

Mr. P. cleared his throat. "The All-Nighter is a wonderful Rotten School tradition," he said. "It started fifty years ago. A man named I.M. Pitiful was headmaster then. His wife had the idea for the party. Her name was Mrs. I.M. Pitiful."

"She liked to stay out all night, prowling on her hands and knees in the grass, looking for field mice and other rodents," Mrs. Pocketlint said. "I don't think she ate them. I think she just liked to catch them."

"She wasn't crazy," Mr. P. said. "It was a hobby. We all have hobbies, right? For example, I like to collect my own toenail clippings. I have two thousand of them in a jar in my room. I give each one a name. Nothing strange about that."

A hushed silence fell over the auditorium. *Toenail clippings?*

"One night Mrs. I.M. Pitiful decided that maybe Rotten School's fourth, fifth, and sixth graders would like to stay out all night hunting rodents, too," Mrs. P. said. "She decided it would be a girl-ask-boy rodent hunt. And that's how the All-Nighter began."

"It was a lot of fun," her husband added. "Because no hands were allowed. You had to use your teeth."

They both chuckled.

We all stared at them. No one made a sound.

Mr. Pocketlint blew his nose loudly again. Then for a few moments he studied what he had done in his handkerchief. "Of course, we don't have a rodent hunt any longer," he said. "The All-Nighter has changed a lot. But it's still a girl-ask-boy party."

Mrs. Pocketlint held up a long sheet of paper. "We have a list of rules you need to follow at the party," she said, sniffing the air again. "The list is short, only one hundred and twelve rules, and I'd like to read them to you now."

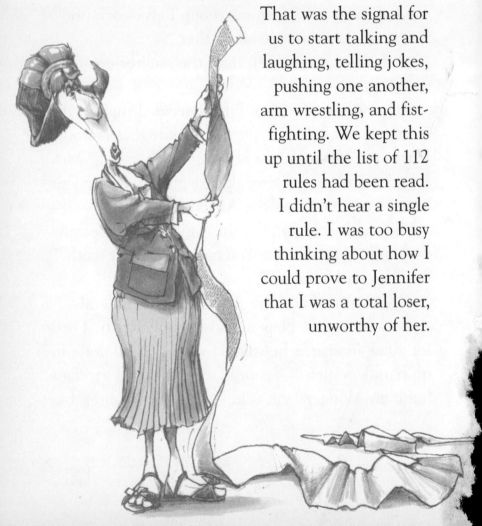

That was the signal for us to start talking and laughing, telling jokes, pushing one another, arm wrestling, and fist-fighting. We kept this up until the list of 112 rules had been read. I didn't hear a single rule. I was too busy thinking about how I could prove to Jennifer that I was a total loser, unworthy of her.

And when I saw Mr. and Mrs. Pocketlint wheel a machine onstage, I realized I had my chance.

I saw my archenemy, that spoiled rich kid, Sherman Oaks, strut onto the stage. Sherman is the leader of Nyce House. He is tall and blond and good-looking, in an icky sort of way.

He's so spoiled, he never looks in a mirror. He has someone *else* look in a mirror for him!

Sherman had a big, toothy grin on his face as he stepped up to the machine. The machine had a flat-screen monitor, a big speaker, and a micro-phone resting on its top.

"Dudes, you probably

know what this is," Sherman said. "But, of course, you're not filthy rich like me, so you can't afford one!"

Mrs. Pocketlint sniffed the air. "Just tell them what it is, Sherman," she said.

"It's a video karaoke machine!" Sherman announced. "We're gonna use it for the All-Nighter."

"YEAAAAAAAA!"

Everyone went nuts. Who doesn't love video karaoke? Sherman Oaks was a hero!

"My parents bought this for me," Sherman announced. "They like to spoil me rotten because then they don't have to spend any time with me!"

"YEAAAA! SHOW US HOW IT WORKS!"

"TRY IT! TRY IT!"

"DO IT, DUDE! BREAK IT DOWN!"

Kids started to scream and shout.

"Do we have a volunteer?" Mrs. Pocketlint shouted.

I jumped to my feet. Perfect! This was my big chance! My chance to look like a total loser in front of Jennifer!

Chapter 12

TINKLE TINKLE

Don't think it's easy for the great Bernie B. to act like a klutz and a loser. I've been a winner all my life, but now I had to act, act, *act*.

I made my way up the stairs to the stage—and stumbled and tripped just to make myself look like a jerk. I flashed Sherman a grin as I stepped up to his machine.

"Ooh, can I try it, Sherman?" I asked, pretending to tremble and shake. "I've never done anything like this before," I said. "Is it hard to do?"

"Go, Bernie!" a girl in the audience shouted.

Who was it? I hoped it wasn't Jennifer.

"Go, Bernie! Go, Bernie!" some other kids started to chant.

I picked up the microphone. "Could you show me how it works?" I asked Sherman. "I'm not a good singer, but perhaps …"

Sherman grinned. "Anyone can do it, Bernie— even you." He turned to the machine and clicked a few dials and buttons.

I pretended to be totally confused. "Do I press this button right here?" I pushed a red button, and a deafening squeal came out of the box.

"No! Don't push that one!" Sherman cried.

"You mean *this* one?" I said. I pushed it again. Another high squeal that made everyone cover their ears.

"Don't touch anything," Sherman said.

"Then how is he going to learn?" Mrs. Pocketlint asked.

"Yes, how am I going to learn?" I said. "Do I turn this?" I reached into an opening on the side of the video screen. "Hey—my hand is stuck!" I cried.

I pretended I couldn't get my hand out. I twisted

and pulled. I pushed the red button again and made the machine squeal.

"Don't touch that!" Sherman cried. He was starting to get steamed.

I heard kids laughing. Some kids still chanted, "Go, Bernie! Go, Bernie!" But now they were being funny. They didn't mean it.

Jennifer, I hope you're watching, I thought. I hope you see what a klutz I am. I hope you're deciding right *now that you can do better than me!*

"Where do I find the songs?" I asked Sherman. "It's so confusing. Do I look in here?"

And I stuck my head into the space between the video screen and the control box.

"Not there! No! Don't do that!" Sherman screamed.

Kids were laughing and hooting.

"My head is stuck!" I cried. "Help me! I can't get my head out!"

Sherman grabbed me by the shoulders and gave me a hard tug.

My head popped out—and the whole karaoke machine fell over and crashed to the floor. *Tinkle tinkle.* Glass flew everywhere. The video screen shattered into a million pieces.

"Oops," I said. "Did I do that?"

I tiptoed off the stage. Kids were muttering and booing and hissing. I looked like a total jerk. But it was for a good cause.

I waited outside the auditorium with my fingers crossed. This *had* to work.

Kids started streaming out. The assembly was

over. I saw April-May hurry over to Jennifer. I crept up behind them to listen.

"Do you see what a loser Bernie is?" April-May said. "See what a total klutz and jerk he is?"

Yes, yes, YES! You go, girl!

But Jennifer shook her head. "Just because Bernie isn't mechanical doesn't mean he's a loser," she said.

Huh?

"I think Bernie did that for ME," Jennifer told April-May. "He knows I *hate* karaoke!"

I let out a long sigh. My body suddenly felt too heavy to stand. I sank to the ground.

Defeated again. Jennifer just wouldn't give up on me.

What could I do to lose The Ecch?

I needed another idea.

I shut my eyes and thought hard. I thought till sweat poured down my face, and my whole body shook.

Yes! Another idea.

Bernie B. *never* runs out of ideas!

I know what will work, I decided. *I'll totally gross her out. . . .*

Chapter 13

EGG BARF

I suddenly remembered the hard-boiled egg-eating contest. Every year I bet on Beast to gobble down the most eggs. But this year was gonna be different.

This year Bernie B. was going to enter the contest.

I made sure Jennifer and Sharonda knew about it. I wanted them to be there.

"Yo, dudes!" I called to my friends as I met them in the little alley behind the Student Center. We hold the contest there so we won't get caught.

I mean, it probably isn't good for you to eat fifty eggs in three minutes.

The contestants stood against a brick wall. Each one had a helper—someone to keep handing him eggs. I saw Joe Sweety, the big, mean kid from Nyce House. He was chewing on a football, warming up his jaw. (I *told* you he was big and mean!)

Feenman was there, cracking open eggs for Beast. Beast warmed up by eating the *shells*!

I picked up a bucket of eggs and moved next to them. I waved to my friend Crench. "Dude, get over here. Start cracking eggs for me."

He squinted at me. "But aren't you betting on Beast?"

"This year I'm betting on Bernie B.," I said. "There's gonna be a new champ this year! Better bet on *me*, dudes—I'm HUNGRY!"

Sherman Oaks stepped up to start the contest. He raised a gold whistle to his lips. "When I blow the whistle, start eating," he said.

But Jennifer and Sharonda weren't there yet. I had to stall. "Sherman, is that whistle real gold?" I asked.

He nodded. "Yeah. My parents sent it to me. It cost five hundred dollars at Tiffany's. They know that *silver* whistles give me chapped lips."

I fingered the whistle. "How does it work?" I asked. "Do you blow into it? Or is this a *digital* one?" I had my eye out for the girls.

Sherman groaned. "Are you stalling, Bernie? If you don't want to eat eggs, step out!"

I saw Sharonda and Jennifer slip into the alley. "Me, stall?" I said. "Why would I stall? I can eat eggs with my eyes closed."

The girls came closer. Jennifer waved a big paw at

me. "Honey Breath!" she called. "I'm here, Honey Breath!"

"Let's start," I said. "I'm HUNGRY!"

Sherman blew the whistle.

Joe, Beast, and I began shoving eggs into our mouths. Ucch. I tried to chew. It tasted like pillow stuffing.

I began sliding them down my throat *without* chewing. Two . . . three . . . Could I manage four? I *had* to!

Next to me, Beast was shoving eggs into his open mouth three at a time. He made a *glug, glug* sound as egg after egg slid down his throat. Next to him, Joe Sweety had egg smeared all over his face. He was half finished with his first bucket.

Crench handed me another egg. I pushed it into my mouth. The yolk stuck to my tongue. I shoved it down with another egg. *Whooooah.* My stomach started to bubble and churn.

I couldn't believe I was doing this. But it was for a good cause!

Sharonda had her arms crossed in front of her. She rolled her eyes. "You guys are totally disgusting," she said. She turned to Jennifer. "Could it be any more disgusting than this?"

Just as she said that, I bent over and started to HURL my guts out.

A waterfall of yellow egg barf gushed from my open mouth. Wet lumps of egg poured out my nose.

The smelly egg barf puddled over my shoes. It stuck to my cheeks and my chin.

When I finally stopped heaving it up, I raised my head and gave Jennifer a big, yellow grin!

This has *to work!* I told myself. *I'm totally gross and disgusting. This has got to turn Jennifer off.*

I pulled a chunk of egg barf from my nose and gazed at her.

"Bernie is a total competitor," she said to Sharonda. "He always plays to win."

"But, Jen—" Sharonda started to protest.

The Ecch smiled at me. "I really admire someone who takes on a new challenge," she said. She stepped up and began tenderly wiping the gunk off my face with her school scarf.

I picked up the egg bucket and slammed it down over my head.

What do I have to *do* to prove to Jennifer that I'm PITIFUL?

Chapter 14

BA-BOOM! BA-BOOM!

I was acting like a loser for so long, I started to *feel* like one!

Come on, dude. Who is the greatest schemer and plotter on earth? Do I have to answer that? So why couldn't I think of a scheme or plot to get rid of The Ecch?

Defeated. Was Bernie B. actually *defeated*?

I couldn't stand it. During the day I walked around campus with my head down, staring at my shoes. At night I sat for hours gazing at the two big cartons on my floor.

The flashlights. The sweatshirts. They were gonna make me RICH! I had to get to the party. But NOT with Jennifer—with April-May.

Sigh, sigh. Day after day I moped and sighed. My friends weren't used to seeing me like this. I know they missed my funny jokes, my winning smile, my great laugh. But what could I do?

Then, one gray afternoon I was surprised to see April-May June come running across the Great Lawn. "Hi, Bernie. How are you?" She flashed me a smile that sent me stumbling back across the grass.

"Uh...good," I said. My legs started shaking. My chest fluttered. Was she actually being NICE to me?

"Bernie, would you go to the All-Nighter with me?" April-May asked.

"Whuh-whuh-whuh-whuh," I replied. My lips didn't work. They suddenly felt like flapping, rubber balloons.

"I *did* plan to ask Sherman Oaks," she said. "But you're so much cuter."

BA-BOOM! BA-BOOM! BA-BOOM!

My heart was pounding so hard, the buttons on my school blazer popped off. Did April-May *finally*

realize that she was my girlfriend?

"Yes," I said. "Of *course* I'll go to the All-Nighter with you."

"GOTCHA!" a husky voice cried. And Jennifer Ecch jumped out from behind a bush. She let out an angry growl and shook both meaty fists at me.

April-May turned to Jennifer. "See?" she said. "I *told* you Bernie was a creep! *Now* do you finally believe me?"

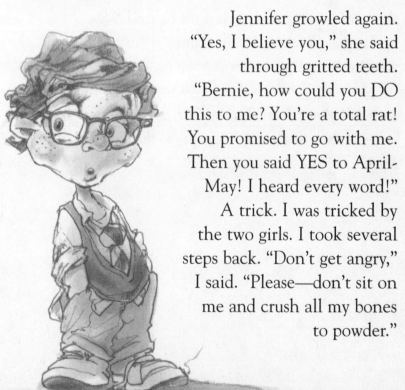

Jennifer growled again. "Yes, I believe you," she said through gritted teeth. "Bernie, how could you DO this to me? You're a total rat! You promised to go with me. Then you said YES to April-May! I heard every word!"

A trick. I was tricked by the two girls. I took several steps back. "Don't get angry," I said. "Please—don't sit on me and crush all my bones to powder."

Jennifer's face turned bright red. "How could you do this? How could you break your promise? You traitor! I'm not taking you to the All-Nighter!" she screamed.

"You-you're not?" I stammered.

"No way. I'm taking back my invitation. I'm going to ask Wes Updood instead," Jennifer said. "Sharonda told me that Wes has a crush on me."

Her size-fourteen shoes pounded the ground as she spun away and hurried off to find Wes.

Is this REALLY happening? I asked myself. I watched Jennifer kick up grass as she ran.

She's going to ask Wes? Did my plan actually work after all? Am I free? Totally FREE?

And does this mean I'm going to the party with April-May?

Chapter 15

"EVERYBODY JOIN IN!"

"Of *course* you're not going with me!" April-May said. She tossed back her head and laughed in my face for nearly ten minutes. "The whole thing was a trick, Bernie. And you fell for it."

She laughed again—until her face turned blue and she had to stop. "I already asked Sherman Oaks," she said, gasping for air. "Bye." She gave me a little wave and trotted off toward the girls' dorm.

Well, I was disappointed that April-May didn't want to ask me. But hey, no biggie. I knew a *dozen* girls were waiting for me. No complaints. Getting rid of The Ecch was a major WIN!

"Sweet!" I cried, clapping my hands together. "Totally sweet!"

I ran all the way to Rotten House, flashing a thumbs-up to every kid I passed. I rushed into my room. "Belzer!" I screamed. "Get in here!"

Belzer came bouncing in from his room across the hall. "What's up, Big B?"

"Open the cartons," I said. "Dust off the flashlights. We're gonna cash in!"

Belzer picked up a flashlight and clicked it five or six times. "But, Bernie, they don't work!" he cried.

"They work fine," I said. "You just have to slap 'em a few times!"

Later, I saw Jennifer and Wes Updood having lunch in the Dining Hall. Jennifer sat really close to Wes and wrapped an arm around his neck. I think she meant it to be friendly. But it looked like a headlock on a TV wrestling smack-down.

She was calling him Honey Cakes and Lamby Breath. Can you *imagine* calling the coolest dude in school "Lamby Breath"?

When she planted loud, smoochy kisses up and down Wes's arm, I had to laugh. "Bernie, you're free!" I told myself. "You're a genius!" I wanted to give MYSELF some smoochy kisses!

Jennifer jumped to her feet. "What can I bring you for lunch, Hot Face?" she shouted.

"Highway 495, exit left onto the interstate," Wes said.

Jennifer nodded. "Do you want ketchup with that?"

"Can you stare into the sun at night?" Wes replied.

"Okay. You got it," Jennifer said. She hurried to the lunch line.

My mouth dropped open. Did she really *understand* what Wes wanted?

I couldn't believe it. Wes and Jennifer were perfect for each other!

Chapter 16

GOOD NEWS, BAD NEWS

The days flew by. The All-Nighter was just a week away. I had good news and bad news.

The good news: Jennifer clung to Wes Updood like a mop on a dust bunny. She followed him everywhere, smothered him with smoochy kisses—and tackled him to the ground whenever he tried to get away.

What a hoot!

Wes was trapped—and I was *free*.

And that's the bad news: I was free. No girl had asked me to the party. I had two cartons of stuff to sell. How could I unload it if I didn't have a date?

Of course, I still hoped April-May would come to her senses and ditch Sherman. But I couldn't count on that.

Why weren't girls lined up to ask me? I *never* like to brag. But I can't tell a lie. Who is the most popular dude at Rotten School? Answer: Bernie B.

Suddenly I knew what the problem was! I just had to let the girls know I was free....

I ran into Flora and Fauna, the Peevish twins, outside the library. I flashed them my most adorable grin, the one with the dimples.

"Don't fight over me, girls," I said. "I know you *both* want me for the All-Nighter. But I don't want to start a battle between sisters. Why don't we just flip a coin?"

"We already asked Feenman and Crench," Flora said.

I patted their heads. "Don't feel bad. I know you're disappointed. Maybe next time."

Sharonda Davis was in the Student Center, playing Ping-Pong with a red-haired girl named Georgia Pines. Sharonda is a tough Ping-Pong player. Her serves flew twenty feet off the table. And poor Georgia had to chase after the ball.

"Sharonda," I said, "all those terrible, gross things you said about me. That was just your cute way of saying you *like* me—right?"

"I asked Joe Sweety to the party," Sharonda said. She slammed the ball into the next room.

I chased after it with Georgia. "You don't know me," I said. "But you are probably *dying* to ask me to the party."

"I asked that cute friend of yours from your dorm," she said.

"Cute friend?"

"Yeah. Nosebleed," she said.

I grabbed the ball and tossed it to her. "Huh? Nosebleed? But he always gets a nosebleed before parties. What if he can't go?"

"He promised me he wouldn't," she said. "He's going to plug up his nose with duct tape just in case."

Good plan.

I slumped back to my room. This was getting *serious*.

Steam poured out when I opened my door. Belzer

was ironing my shirts. "Not too much starch," I said. "You know I have very delicate skin."

Belzer nodded. "No problem, Big B. I walked your dog, and I watered your plants."

Good kid, Belzer.

"Do you have a date to the All-Nighter?" I asked him.

Belzer nodded. "Yeah. Patti Kakes asked me."

My mouth dropped open. "Patti Kakes? But that girl chews on her braids all the time. And she LICKS her textbooks!"

"So what?" Belzer said. "She asked me."

I sighed and dropped onto my bed. Belzer had a date, and I didn't.

What should I do? I needed a plan—*and I didn't have one!*

Chapter 17

JENNIFER CHANGES HER MIND

SHOULD STUDENTS BE ALLOWED TO BRING LAPTOPS TO CLASS?

That was the question the Rotten School Debate Team was arguing. They were debating a team of three kids from Easter Bunny Prep.

The debates are a big deal. All of us fourth graders have to go to them. We piled into the auditorium and took seats way in the back so we could goof around and talk and take naps.

I glanced at the stage. The three kids on our team were Sherman Oaks, Wes Updood, and Georgia

Pines. They were looking through their notes, getting ready to debate. I saw Jennifer Ecch in the front row, blowing kisses to Wes.

Sherman started the debate. He walked to the front of the stage and held up a shiny silver laptop.

"My new laptop has a solid chrome body," he said. "That's so I can see myself as I type on it." He held it higher. "It has leopard skin on all the keys so I don't bruise my fingertips."

He stepped back. "I don't have an argument," he said. "I just wanted to show you the laptop. I know *you* can't afford one this nice."

Wes Updood went next. He studied his note cards for a moment. Then he spoke into the microphone. "George Washington, everyone," he said. "Uncle of our country. Supersize it! Yo!"

Silence in the auditorium. Then Jennifer shouted, "Brilliant! Brilliant! That's so smart!"

"You da man! Give it up!" Wes said, reading his notes. "Save big money now. It's like sliced peaches, ya know?"

"Brilliant!" Jennifer cried. She jumped to her feet and clapped. "Brilliant! Sliced peaches. Why didn't

I think of that? Brilliant!"

"What about laptops?" a kid from Easter Bunny Prep shouted.

"What about your *thumb?*" Wes replied. "Ever suck on it for an hour and then *smell* it?"

Jennifer started to clap again. "Brilliant! Totally brilliant! No way we can lose now!"

No one else had a clue what Wes was talking about. But he talked for another twenty minutes. He was totally cool. So cool, he wasn't even speaking English! Then he picked up his saxophone and started to play.

The debate was over. No one on the other team got to say a word. That's why Rotten School wins every debate.

Wes started to leave the stage. Jennifer hurried up to join him. "Brilliant! Lamby Knees, you're SO SMART!" she cried. She hugged him so hard, I could hear his ribs cracking.

Jennifer, Wes, and Sherman left the auditorium. I followed them. I *loved* seeing Wes smothered by The Ecch.

They made their way to the snack shop at the

Student Center. I followed them as they got in line.

Jennifer had her arm around Wes's shoulders. As they walked, she nibbled on his ear, making loud, slurping noises.

He turned to her. "Marble cheesecake," he said angrily.

Her smile faded. She jerked her arm away. "*What* did you say?"

"Marble cheesecake," Wes repeated. "Strawberry shortcake. You know what I'm talking about. Like elephants on rice."

"How DARE you!" Jennifer screamed. "How DARE you insult my hair like that!"

"Huh?" Wes squinted at her, confused. "Graham cracker crust?" he murmured. "Smell my armpit on your birthday?"

With a roar, Jennifer pounced on him. She knocked him to the floor. "I thought you *liked* me! Why are you saying those horrible things about the way I look?"

"Pony rides, man. Pony rides," Wes said. Then he screamed in pain.

Sherman jumped to rescue his friend. He grabbed

Jennifer by the shoulders and tried to pull her off Wes. Jennifer spun around. Her one brown eye and one blue eye flashed. She stared at Sherman as if she'd never seen him before.

Then she let go of Wes, leaped to her feet—and wrapped her arms around Sherman's waist. "Honey Cakes!" she cried. "You're mine now! MINE!"

"Gulp!" Sherman choked on a big wad of bubble gum. "Excuse me?"

"Honey Cakes!" Jennifer cried. "It's you and me, Shermie! Big-time!"

Sherman made some more gulping sounds. He tried to shove her away with his chrome laptop.

But The Ecch grabbed his left arm and twisted it behind his back. "Promise you'll go to the All-Nighter with me!" she screamed.

"Huh? No way!" Sherman gasped. "OWWWW!"

He screamed as The Ecch twisted his arm higher behind him. "Honey Face," Jennifer cooed, "I won't let go until you promise to go with me."

"But-but-but—" Sherman sputtered.

"OWWWWWWWWWWWW!"

"Is that a yes or a no?" Jennifer asked.

Chapter 18

IN THE SOUP

My buddies Feenman and Crench and I were having lunch in the Dining Hall. I looked up and saw April-May June heading our way.

"I know why she's coming over here," I told them. "Sherman has been captured by The Ecch. So April-May needs a date to the All-Nighter. I won't make her beg for *too* long."

April-May stepped up to our table. Her blond ponytail swung behind her. She kept clenching her fists. "Jennifer ruined everything," she said. "She *knew* Sherman was my date."

I crinkled up my eyes the way that always drives girls crazy. "So you've come to ask me instead?" I said.

April-May spit her gum into my chicken soup. "Bernie," she said, "I'd rather have my tongue pulled out through my nose."

I laughed. "You're a great kidder. Yes, I'll go with you."

She clamped a hand onto my shoulder. "You have to get Jennifer back," she said. "You have to fix this. You have to get her back so I can go with Sherman."

"Get her BACK? *No way!*" I cried. "It took me *months* to get rid of her!"

April-May shrugged. "Then you won't have a date for the party, Bernie. You'll be sitting by yourself in your room—with those two big cartons."

I swallowed. "And I'll be totally broke?"

April-May nodded.

I let out a sigh. "Maybe you have a point," I said. "But how can I get Jennifer back? The party is tomorrow night."

"You'll think of something," April-May said. She patted me on the shoulder and hurried away.

I shook my head sadly. Get The Ecch back? *Don't even* think *about it!* I told myself. But, did I have a choice?

"Wow," Feenman said. "April-May had a weird way of begging you."

Crench had his eyes on my soup bowl. "Bernie,

do you want that?" he asked.

"No. Take it," I said.

He reached into the soup, pulled out April-May's gum, and popped it into his mouth.

Chapter 19

"MMMMWWWWW-AAAAAAAAH!"

Chills ran down my back. I shook. I staggered. My eyes bulged. My tongue hung out of my mouth and wagged like a dog's tail. My whole head shook like a bobblehead doll's.

But I had no choice. I had to get The Ecch back before tomorrow night. And I knew how to do it.

Jennifer *loved* it when I acted like a creep and a klutz and a jerk. She thought that was the BEST. No matter what I did, she thought it was awesome.

All I had to do was repeat all those creepy, klutzy, jerky things. I knew I'd have her back in no time.

I rounded up the first-grade kids again. I waited for Jennifer to walk by Rotten House with Sherman. And I dropped water balloons onto the little kids.

Leaning out my dorm window, I saw Jennifer turn to Sherman. "Bernie is *so* immature," she said. "*You'd* never do anything like that, Shermie Pie." They kept walking.

Strike one. That didn't work. No prob!

I remembered how Jennifer liked it when I stuck my head into Sherman's karaoke machine and wrecked it. I found Sherman onstage in the auditorium. Jennifer was watching him repair the machine.

"Hey, guys," I said, climbing onstage. "Here, Sherman. Let Bernie B. give you a hand. I know just how to fix these things."

I fiddled with some dials. Then I stuck my head inside the machine again. "Help! I'm stuck! I'm stuck!" That *had* to win Jennifer back.

"Bernie, how can you be such a total spaz?" she snarled. She tugged my head free, then gave me a boot in the butt that sent me flying into the seats. "Get lost!"

Okay, okay. Strike two.

But, no prob. I still had the hard-boiled-egg-eating contest. Jennifer went nuts for that. I remembered how it totally impressed her.

The guys didn't want to do another egg-eating contest. They said they were still urping up egg from the last one. I had to bribe them with free flashlights and sweatshirts.

We got ready in the alley behind the Student Center. As soon as I saw Jennifer coming, I started stuffing eggs down my throat.

"MMMMWWWW~ AAAAAAAAH!"

I threw up all over my own shoes. Yellow chunks poured from my mouth and nose. I waited for Jennifer to hurry over to help me.

"Ooh, totally gross!" she cried, holding her nose. "Bernie, why don't you *grow up?*" She turned and galloped away.

"Oh, wow. *That* went well," I muttered. I stared down at the yellow glop on my shoes.

Strike three. Bernie is out.

My shoes made squishy sounds as I trudged back to Rotten House. I didn't care. I failed to get Jennifer back. I knew that tomorrow I'd be doing an all-nighter—alone in my room!

Chapter 20

A Deadly Tug of War

The All-Nighter started with a barbeque blowout in the Dining Hall. Chef Baloney and his helpers stood beside huge barbeque grills. They served up *tons* of smoking hot dogs, burgers, chicken, and ribs.

I gazed around the brightly decorated hall. The theme of this year's party was "Pond Life." Giant lily pads and paper pond scum hung from the rafters. And some awesome artist had painted a huge mural of snails and leeches and fish skeletons.

"Totally excellent!" I exclaimed to April-May as we stepped into the line for food.

"Don't talk to me," she said. "Pretend you're not with me."

Well, I know. You're probably wondering what Bernie B. was doing at the party. And how I got there with April-May June.

Simple. About ten minutes before the party started, April-May realized that she and I were the only ones without dates. So she came to see me.

I could tell she was *crazy* about me. "Bernie," she said, "I'd rather hammer rusty nails into my ears. But what choice do I have? I have to ask you to the All-Nighter."

Yes! YES! Sweet!

What a night for the great Bernie B.! I'm at the party with the coolest, hottest girl in school. I'm gonna GET RICH QUICK with my flashlights and sweatshirts. AND Sherman Oaks is stuck with The Ecch.

Could life *get* any sweeter?

"Enjoy your dinners, everyone!" Mrs. Pocketlint shouted. She and Mr. Pocketlint stood at a microphone in the front of the hall. "Don't eat *too* much. You want to be light and fast for the soccer game, the three-legged race across Pooper's Pond, and the treasure hunt."

At the end of our table, my buddies Feenman and Crench were tossing chicken wings back and forth, catching them in their *teeth*. Those two dudes know how to *party!*

April-May stood up and shouted to everyone, "I'm not really here with Bernie! I know it *looks* like I'm here with Bernie. But I'm not."

She's so cute.

I raised my cheeseburger to my mouth. But I didn't get to take a bite. Because I felt a hard tap on my shoulder.

I spun around. "Jennifer? What do you want?"

"I changed my mind," she said. "You're *my* date now."

I dropped the cheeseburger. "Are you crazy?" I cried. "It's too late. The party started already. Go back to Sherman."

"It's never too late," Jennifer cooed, "when a girl is in love." She started licking the back of my neck.

"Yuck!" I groaned. "Get that cow tongue off me!

Jennifer, why are you doing this?"

She grinned. Her one brown eye and one blue eye sparkled. "See what Sherman gave me? He said I could have this if I went back to you." She held up a hundred-dollar bill.

April-May gasped. She stared at the money. "Jennifer," she said, "you can't let a boy bribe you like that."

"Sure, I can!" Jennifer said. She bent down and started licking my neck again.

April-May grabbed my left arm. "I don't want to be here with Bernie," she told Jennifer. "I'd rather have huge purple spots all over my body. But—this isn't *fair!*"

"Let go of him!" Jennifer cried. She grabbed my right arm. "Sherman gave me a hundred dollars to go back to Bernie. And that's what I'm going to do."

"No, you're not!" April-May screamed. She pulled my arm as hard as she could.

"Give him to me!" Jennifer grunted. She pulled my other arm with all her strength.

Tug-of-war time, dudes.

Does it look like I might be in trouble here?

Chapter 21

RUINED!

"Don't fight over me, girls," I said. "I know I'm fabulous, but give me a break here. Maybe you could *share!*"

"No way!" they both screamed, tugging harder. I heard my armpits crack! If something didn't happen soon, they'd *pull me apart!*

"Listen up, everyone!" Mr. Pocketlint shouted. "Time for the annual three-legged race! Everyone outside! Line up at Pooper's Pond!"

Chairs scraped. Kids started to run out of the Dining Hall. I thought this might save me. But I was wrong.

I staggered to the door with both girls pulling me from side to side. It was a clear, cool night. A silvery moon shone down, floating just above the trees.

But I couldn't enjoy it. The two girls wouldn't stop their tug-of-war. My arms were already eight feet long!

No one knows how Pooper's Pond got its name. Maybe it's the smell. Maybe it's because the water is thick and lumpy.

A narrow, wooden bridge stretches over the pond. The three-legged race starts at the bridge. I saw kids pairing up and pulling burlap bags over their middle legs.

Belzer stood beside the bridge. He was leaning on one of my two cartons. Jennifer pulled me toward Belzer. April-May tugged me away.

"Belzer, quick—" I shouted. "Get the cartons open. We've gotta sell, sell, SELL!"

April-May let go of me for a moment to pick up a burlap bag. I grabbed a handful of flashlights from the carton. Jennifer started to pull a bag up over my left leg.

"Flashlights!" I shouted, waving them in the air.

"They're only a dollar. How else can you see where you're running? Flashlights, everyone!"

April-May struggled to pull a bag up onto my right leg.

"You girls can't do this!" I cried. "It's not a six-legged race!" I waved the flashlights. "Only a dollar! I have change for bigger bills!" I shouted.

The girls were tugging up the burlap bags. "Give me a break!" I said. "I've gotta sell this stuff!"

"Bernie, get away from the boxes," Jennifer growled. "We have to race."

"No!" April-May protested. "WE have to race."

"Flashlights!" I called. "Sweatshirts! Who's cold? Who needs a sweatshirt?"

"You're RUINING the race!" Jennifer cried. She let go of me, but she dove at the two cartons.

"Jennifer—don't!" I cried.

She lifted both cartons above her head—and HEAVED them over the side of the bridge—into Pooper's Pond!

"NOOOO!"

I screamed. "That's *three months'* allowance!"

I didn't think. I took a deep breath, broke away from both girls—and *dove* into the water after my cartons.

SPLAAAAAT!

I hit bottom, then came floating back up, covered in muck and brown, lumpy water. "My sweatshirts! My flashlights! My MONEY!" I wailed.

But the cartons had sunk to the bottom.

RUINED.

I was RUINED.

I slapped the thick, chunky water with both hands. Then I slapped it again.

"He's DROWNING!" I heard Jennifer shout. "Don't worry, Bernie. I'll save you!"

I saw April-May racing away, crossing the bridge—with Sherman! What a traitor!

And then there was a huge

SPLASH!

Smelly, thick water washed over me. Jennifer popped up at my side. She wrapped an arm around my neck and started dragging me toward shore.

My mouth filled with the pukey water. I started to choke.

Jennifer grinned at me. "This is the most *awesome* party!" she gushed. "I can't believe we get to do this ALL NIGHT!"

"My money . . ." I muttered. "My money . . . I'm broke. . . . I'm busted. . . ."

SOB!
SOB!

The disgusting, brown water was caked in my hair. It oozed down my face. I blinked. Someone was shining a light into my eyes.

I glanced up at the bridge—and saw Belzer holding a flashlight.

He grinned down at me. "Bernie, I saved one!"
he called. "Can I keep it?"

A BAD
ALLERGY

The boy pulled a sweater from his suitcase and care-fully folded it. He flashed me another smile. "I'm Angel Goodeboy," he said again. He walked over and shook my hand.

What was *up* with this guy? I stared at him. I'd never met a kid who shook hands before!

"Well, I'm sorry, dude," I said. "But you're in the wrong room. I'm Bernie Bridges. This is my room."

His cheeks turned bright red. He really *did* look like an angel. He just needed a halo and he'd be perfect.

"I'm in the wrong room?" he gasped. "Oh, my

HERE'S A SNEAK PEEK AT BOOK #10

R.L. STINE'S

ROTTEN SCHOOL

The Rottenest Angel

gosh and goodness! I'm so sorry. Mrs. Heinie showed me in here."

"I guess Mrs. Heinie didn't clean her glasses this morning," I said.

Mrs. Heinie is our fourth-grade teacher and dorm mother. She is so nearsighted, she can't find her nose without a map!

"She made a mistake," I said. "Let me help you get packed up again."

"Oh, my gosh and goodness! I'm so, so, so sorry," he said. "I hope you will forgive me."

"No problem," I said. "Just pack up your stuff. Maybe you could share the room across the hall with Feenman, Crench, and Belzer. There's plenty of room over there."

I heard footsteps in the hall, then a voice in the doorway. "Oh. Have you two boys met?" I turned to see Mrs. Heinie peering at us through her thick glasses.

I flashed her my best smile. "Mrs. Heinie, you're looking wonderful!" I said. "That red bracelet on your arm—is it new? Very pretty!"

"I'm not wearing a red bracelet," she said. "I have a skin rash."

"Well, it looks very nice on you," I said. "I'm just

3

helping the new kid pack up. He's in the wrong room."

Angel clasped his chubby little hands together. "I'm so, so, so, so sorry," he said. "I don't want to crowd Bernie's space."

Mrs. Heinie made a choking sound. "He's in the right room, Bernie. You'll just have to learn to *share*."

"But—But—But—" I sputtered.

I pulled Mrs. H. into the hall. "You *know* I can't have a roommate," I whispered to her. "I brought a doctor's note. I'm allergic."

I sneezed as hard as I could.

Mrs. Heinie wiped off the front of her sweater.

"See?" I said. "That Angel kid is making me sneeze already!"

I grabbed my neck. "My throat—it's closing up," I whispered. "Hard to breathe. I'm allergic to room-mates. You understand, right?"

Mrs. Heinie stepped back into the room. Angel was waiting patiently, hands in his khaki pockets.

"Angel is staying," Mrs. H. said. "I put him in here, Bernie, because I hope a little bit of his *goodness* will rub off on you!"

Angel's eyes twinkled. I'm not sure how he made

them twinkle like that. He flashed us another angelic smile.

"Mrs. H., please—" I begged. "I'm allergic to that smile! Look. It's making me ITCH all over!" I started scratching my whole body.

Mrs. Heinie scowled at me. "I don't want any trouble from you," she growled. "And don't try to teach him any of your sneaky tricks. He's a *good* boy, and he'd better stay that way!"

Angel's little red mouth formed a pout. "Oh, my gosh and goodness. I'm sorry if you don't want me, Bernie," he said in a soft, sad voice. "I'll stay out of your way. I'll stay in that corner over there." He pointed.

"Tell you what," he said. "I'll sleep in the closet. And in the morning I'll get dressed out in the hall. You won't even see me."

Mrs. Heinie squinted at me. "Do you see what an *angel* he is? See how kind and generous?"

I started scratching my chest and arms. "Mrs. H., check it out. He's making me ITCH again! Please— he has to go!"

I had to do something. *No way* I could share my room with an *angel!*

But what could I do?

ABOUT THE AUTHOR

R.L. Stine graduated from Rotten School with a solid D+ average, which put him at the top of his class. He says that his favorite activities at school were Scratching Body Parts and Making Armpit Noises.

In sixth grade, R.L. won the school Athletic Award for his performance in the Wedgie Championships. Unfortunately, after the tournament, his underpants had to be surgically removed.

After graduation, R.L. became well known for writing scary book series such as The Nightmare Room, Fear Street, Goosebumps, and Mostly Ghostly, and a short story collection called *Beware!*

Today, R.L. lives in New York City, where he is busy writing stories about his school days.

For more information about R.L. Stine,
go to www.rottenschool.com
and www.rlstine.com